J
KRAUS
KRAUS, JEANNE

GET READY FOR JETTY MY
JOURNAL ABOUT ADHD AND ME

Get Ready for Jetty

Published by
MAGINATION PRESS
An Educational Publishing Foundation Book
American Psychological Association
750 First Street, NE
Washington, DC 20002

For more information about our books, including a complete catalog, please write to us, call 1-800-374-2721, or visit our website at www.apa.org/pubs/magination.

Cover and book design by Sandra Kimbell
Printed by Worzalla, Stevens Point, WI

Library of Congress Cataloging-in-Publication Data
Kraus, Jeanne R., date.
  Get ready for Jetty : my journal about ADHD and me / by Jeanne Kraus ; design and decorations by Sandra Kimbell.
      p. cm.
  "American Psychological Association."
  Summary: "Tells the story of Jetty, a girl with ADHD. With the help of her doctor, counselor, teacher, and parents, she is able to overcome her problems at school and with friends"—Provided by publisher.
  ISBN 978-1-4338-1196-8 (hardcover : alk. paper) — ISBN 978-1-4338-1197-5 (pbk. : alk. paper) [1. Hyperactive children—Fiction. 2. Attention-deficit hyperactivity disorder—Fiction. 3. Schools—Fiction. 4. Diaries—Fiction.] I. Kimbell, Sandra, ill. II. Title.
  PZ7.K8673Ge 2012
  [Fic]—dc23
                              2012019115

        0 1021 0286105 5

Manufactured in the United States of America

First printing — June 2012

10 9 8 7 6 5 4 3 2 1

green circle
USA
ECO-FRIENDLY BOOKS
Made in the USA

Get Ready for Jetty

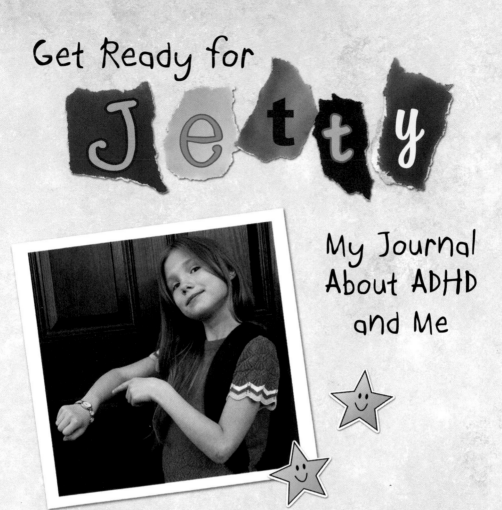

My Journal
About ADHD
and Me

by Jeanne Kraus

design and decorations
by Sandra Kimbell

Magination Press ● Washington, DC
American Psychological Association

August 15

The *first* Day!

Yay! School is here.
New teacher = Mrs. Taylor.
Hope she likes me.

This year,
I will find a
best friend.

Good-bye, boring
old nothing-to-do
summer!

Ready...Set...

JETTY!

Jetty Lynn Carmichael

9 1/2 years old
Fourth Grade

Happy First Day!
See Ya at 3.

— Love, Mom

Exciting!

Hurray!

Fun!

School Supplies Needed

- 1 glue stick
- 6 sharp pencils
- 1 red pencil
- 1 pair of scissors
- 1 box of markers
- 1 box of colored pencils
- notebook paper
- 6 folders with pockets
- 1 ruler
- 1 box of 16 crayons

- 1 sparkly pencil

75¢

—— Gazette Daily News

WANTED: BEST FRIEND
Fun and good at cartwheels
See Jetty! Room 151

School, here I come

August 20

Fourth grade is a little bit hard!
I miss third grade. It wasn't so boring.

Mrs. Taylor is making us keep a Fourth Grade Journal.
She likes us to write stuff about our day.
And our thoughts.

Here is my first thought:

> My journal can be in non-cursive. Yay!

⊚ FOURTH GRADE = WEIRD! ⊚

#1 Reason! We have to sit forever.
   I want to spring out of my seat. My legs and arms have tickles and itches. All of me wants to **move!**

#2 Reason! There's too much work.

I mean TONS of work. Truckloads even.
Just my heading takes forever. My papers look messy.
My eraser makes holes in my paper.

My Favorite Memory

> How do the other kids get it done?

#3 Reason! The teacher talks ALL DAY!

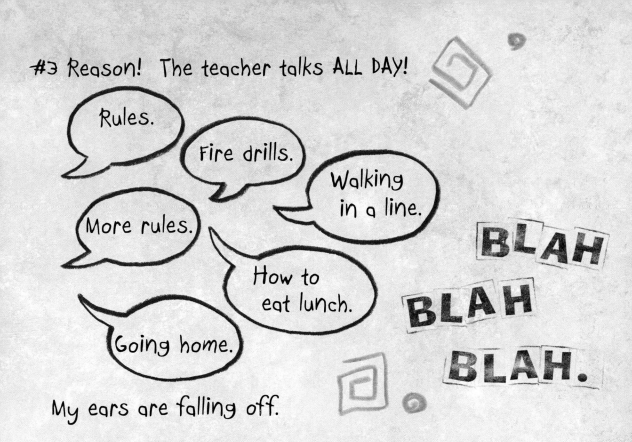

Rules.

Fire drills.

Walking in a line.

More rules.

How to eat lunch.

Going home.

BLAH BLAH BLAH.

My ears are falling off.

#4 Reason! I am starving.

My stomach is rumbling growly noises.

Growl! Rumble! Urble! Glurk!

I want my turkey sandwich.
And my chocolate chip cookies.

Finally I'm just about dead.
Then we go to lunch.
I should win first prize for the fastest eater.

 Is this how the whole year will be?

September 3

I have to say...

School is way too much writing!

I have a mountain of work to do.
Only me.
No one else has a pile of
work all over THEIR desk.

And some papers under it.

 Is that fair?

plus there are too many rules in fourth grade.

A **GAZILLION** Rules

Mrs. Taylor handed out these.

Mrs. Taylor's Rules for Fourth Grade

1. Use inside voices.
2. Keep hands to yourself.
3. Be a good listener.
4. Raise hand to speak.
5. Finish work.

I wish I could make the rules.

Jetty's Rules for Fourth Grade

1. Never write in complete sentences. It wastes time.
2. Teachers need to talk about cool stuff so kids listen.
3. Kids need exercise. Make recess longer.
4. Kids need more talking time in school.
5. No homework on school nights. Or weekends.
6. Everyone gets to use a computer to type homework.

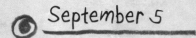
September 5

Classroom jobs are assigned today.
Guess which one I got?

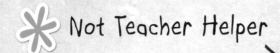 Not Teacher Helper

* Not Line Leader

* Not Messenger

my #1
favorite

my #2
favorite

my tied-for
#1 favorite

I have to be Floor Sweeper.

AAACK!   I hate Floor Sweeper.

It's almost as terrible as Table Washer.

More bad news for me.
We have to write in complete sentences.

My writing stinks. I need a fourth grade secretary.

———— Gazette Daily News

NOW HIRING: 4th grade secretary.
Must be able to write in complete
sentences. See Jetty, room 151.

Why do we have to write everything? Can we just say
the answers?

?????

I know the answers.

We could cooperate and make school easier.

September 10

Here are some
things I know.

Name Jetty Lynn Carmichael

MATH

5 TIMES TABLE

5 x 1   = 5
5 x 2   = 10
5 x 3   = 15
5 x 4   = 20
5 x 5   = 25
5 x 6   = 30
5 x 7   = 35
5 x 8   = 40
5 x 9   = 45
5 x 10 = 50

 Words I can spell...
Mississippi
Camouflage

Jetty's Favorite Facts
• Newborn kangaroos are 1 inch long.
• Rats can't throw up.
• An ostrich eye is bigger than
  its brain.
• Baby beavers are called kittens.
• Tigers have striped skin, not just
  striped fur.

COOL!

WOW!

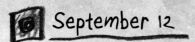

I always have to sit near the teacher.
 Ever since I was a kid, that's where I've had to sit.

 Me and Jordan
    ALWAYS
    ———
    sit by the teacher.

Next to the window is better. It's not boring there.
I can see the playground.

A seat with a good view. That's all I ask.

Life = Unfairness = Horrible, Super Bad Day!

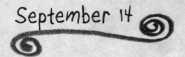

September 14

Everyone bothers me. For no reason.

I am so starving
I almost do a
hungry faint in
the lunch line.

Then Casey cuts in front of me.
I push her. (By accident.) *

The hungriest kid in the class (me)
had to go to the way end of the line.

Practically all the way
to Kansas I think.

(The lunch lady never listens to
my side of what happens.)

September 17

Robbie hogs the good markers. I make him share.

The Marker Hog

But guess
who gets
in trouble?

Rules work for
other kids,
never for me.

I get blamed for
EVERYTHING.

Sometimes I get so mad I cry. That's embarrassing.

The whole class stares at me.

Sometimes I just quit talking to everyone.

No Offense, but WRITING is a major Time Sucker.

 Who invented complete sentences, anyway?

A teacher who hates kids, maybe.

 My Least Favorite Teacher Comments on my Papers

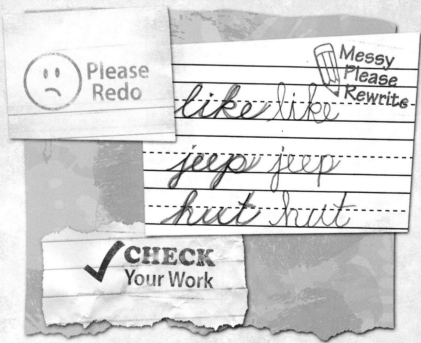

Writing in cursive is SO NOT creative.
So NOT me.

September 20

I don't get it! If the answers are right...
   Who cares about handwriting?

Writing in cursive
  takes me millions
of hours each week.

*

This Week's Count:

3 5, 7 6 8, 4 3 2

I could be doing fun stuff with those million hours.

Fun stuff like:
- Movies
- Parties
- Roller skating
- Riding my bike

TICKET
ADMIT ONE
880262

September 24

I can't get any work done.

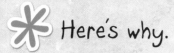 Here's why.

> Brent sharpens his pencil.
>   Over and over and over and over.

The rule says no pencil sharpening during reading.

I raise my hand to tell on Brent but Mrs. Taylor gives me the T.E. (teacher eyeball.) That means Get To Work!

I try to concentrate. Really try.

But Jordan has such cool sneakers.

COOL!

I need new sneakers. Hint, Mom!

Sam's finger is always in his nose.
Today it's the left nostril.

EEUW!........

Eeuw! Gross! I say Sam needs
to keep his hands to himself.

Gross!

Gag!

...Whoosh!

The toilet is flushing again.
Whoosh! Whoosh! Really? Again? Whoosh!
These kids drink way too much water.

||| Distractions Are Denying Me An Education!!! |||

No wonder I have total Brain Drain.

SHARPENING!   PICKING!

FLUSHING!   I need HELP!

S.O.S.

October 1

Mom needs to remember I am SO not a morning person.
6:30 am: Stomach still asleep. Eating is torture.

 B is for Breakfast.

Also Barf.

After breakfast...a whole family scavenger hunt.
We look for my math book and my right shoe.

It is my fault we are late to
school again. Everyone reminds me.

Everything is my fault.

 Barfy Morning = Super Terrible Day!

I forget my math homework and my lunchbox.

I have to buy a cafeteria lunch.
Rubber Grilled Cheez Sandwich.
Only skim milk is left.

Yecch!

Is this brain food?
Really?

Washington Elementary
WE make the grade!

OCTOBER
Lunch Menu

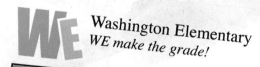

MONDAY	TUESDAY	WEDNESDAY	THURSDAY	FRIDAY
1 Grilled Cheese Sandwich Vegetable Soup Apple Milk Selection	2 Beef Burrito Steamed Rice Fruit Cup Milk Selection	3 Cheese Ravioli Roll Grapes Milk Selection	4 Cheeseburger on a Bun Mixed Vegetables Apple Milk Selection	FALL FESTIVA Popcorn Chic Roll Corn Milk Selectio
8 Pizza Salad Applesauce Milk Selection Columbus Day	9 Oriental Chicken Rice Steamed Broccoli Milk Selection	10 Corn Dog Nuggets Roll Pear Slices Milk Selectio	11 Macaroni & Cheese Mixed Vegetable Banana	Chili with Bee Rol
15				

Worst of all my favorite sparkly pencil is missing.

Something else bad...

We changed classroom jobs.
Now I'm the Table Washer.

Jetty's Jobs	Good Jobs
• Table Washer • Floor Sweeper	• Everything Else

My whole day is RUINED!

PS. My Work Mountain
is about one foot taller.

October 4

 News—An envelope for
Mom and Dad.

You know what
that means.

Conference Time.

I'd rather go to
the doctor and get
a shot. Maybe.

To the parents of
JETTY LYNN CARMICHAEL

I WAS BRAVE TODAY!
I had a shot!

plus I still don't have a best friend.

 What's
up with
that?

Please Check Box.

I like Jetty.
☐ Yes   ☐ No

Does anyone have such horrible days as me?

October 5

⭐ Tonight is Fall Festival Night!

fall
FESTIVAL

October 5th
5:00-7:00 p.m.

- games
- prizes
- refreshments
- face painting
- and more!

Tickets
$1 each

WE Washington Elementary
WE make the grade!

All day I think of...

- Popcorn
- Cotton Candy
- Cake Walk
- Penny candy
- Face Painting
  (I want to be a pirate)
- Hot dogs and pizza.

I can't wait.

Mrs. Taylor keeps telling me to FOCUS.
I am. Just not on school.

October 15

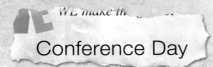

Conference Day

Mom and Dad see my papers.
 The good ones. And not-so-good ones.
They even check my desk. My personal space.

Mom says she felt dizzy from the mess.
Sometimes she can be a Drama Queen.

Mrs. Taylor says I need help.

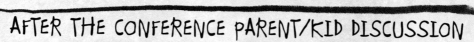

AFTER THE CONFERENCE PARENT/KID DISCUSSION

GOOD THINGS

- Mom and Dad are not mad.
- They know I'm trying.
- I'm smart.
- They found my missing
  library book in my desk!
  (but no sparkly pencil!)

NOT SO GOOD THINGS

- My grades
- I need to be a good
  friend to others
- Listening
- Following directions
- Organization

NOT SURE THINGS

- Going to a doctor
- Visiting Mrs. B, our school counselor
- Homework buddy
- Study plan

Whew!

At least Mom and Dad didn't take me out of karate.
I was worried.
Karate is amazing.

KAIMU'S KARATE

Classes for • ADULTS
          • CHILDREN 3 yrs & older
$40 per month
ask about our Family Discount!

First Class
FREE!

LandsEnd Shopping Center
555-0126

I met a karate friend named Mandy.

She's not a girlie-girl.
Just bouncy like me.

We might get our
yellow belts soon!

Today was the Character Parade.

All the kids and teachers dress up as their favorite book character.

Mine is Katie Kazoo Switcheroo.
My karate stuff is perfect for Karate Katie.

Guess What?

I go to school.
All my karate stuff is still at home. Somewhere.
The parade is almost starting.

 Meltdown Alert!! My teacher finds a t-shirt for me to wear. She says Katie Kazoo would like it.

I don't think so. Katie is very picky.

She gives me the Karate Katie book to carry.
I have to parade in a not-so-Katie Kazoo shirt.

I kick rocks as we walk.
Stupid shirt. Dumb parade.

October 29

Mrs. Taylor thinks it is a good time for me to talk to the counselor.

Mrs. B asks me about my feelings.

I'm mad. That's what.

No one reminded me to bring my karate stuff.

Where's your family when you need them?

Mrs. B says I should write it down in my agenda. And put it in the "To School" bin by the door.

She is going to help me be more organized.

TOO LATE NOW.

I'm not Katie Kazoo any more.

November 1

I have a new doctor. Her name is Dr. Petrie.

She's going to find out what's going on with me.

FAMILY MEDICAL CLINIC
Isabel Petrie, MD

Jetty Lynn
has an appointment
MON   TUES   WED   THUR   (FRI)   SAT
November 2   at   *4:30 pm*
40 Washington Square WILDWOOD 555-0189

Like those problems that are bugging me at school.

OK.

I'm ready for some good days. So are Mom and Dad. Mrs. Taylor sure is ready.

They filled out some papers all about me.

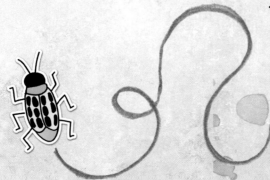

November 2

Guess WHAT? Dr. Petrie tells me I have ADHD!
I don't think so. I want a second opinion.

 I know all about ADHD. My cousin Bryan is ADHD.
   ● He runs around.   ● He gets in fights.
   ● He acts kind of goofy sometimes.

 I am not like Bryan.
   ● I can focus on TV shows. ● I'm good at karate.
   ● I know my math facts. ● I can read really fast.

But then
Dr. Petrie shows
me a list.

Wow!

This does kind of
sound like Jetty Lynn
Carmichael (me).

(I don't really have
trouble keeping friends.
I just can't find any.)

FAMILY MEDICAL CLINIC
40 Washington Square WILDWOOD 555-0189
Isabel Petrie, MD

ADHD checklist

- Problems with organization
- Restless and "on the go"
- Easily distracted
- Difficulty with focusing on
  less preferred tasks
- Difficulties maintaining friendships
- Speaks/acts before thinking
- Difficulty with time management

But how will this list help me?

Mom said it made her feel better.
She said the pieces of the Jetty
Jigsaw finally got put together.
I don't know what she means by that.

I'm not a puzzle.

But everyone else sure is.

I will think about this ADHD stuff some more.

Mom reminds me I'm not the only one. Other kids have ADHD.

Guess what? Jordan said he is ADHD. I never knew that.

Some adults have ADHD.
Even Dr. Petrie. And she's an expert.

She will help me with problems at school and home.

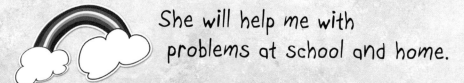

November 5

I'm so over problems. No one in the world
has as many as me.

Why am I so different?
Can't I just be a kid?

* I don't want to have ADHD. Even if Jordan does.

OK I even cried a little. Cause life should be fair.
Either everyone should be ADHD.
Or no one should be ADHD.

OH WOW!

What if everyone in the whole wide world
itched and twitched
and didn't focus
and was disorganized?

The world would
be in big trouble. **HUGE!**

Mom says we are all different
and that makes life interesting.

Well I know one thing for sure.

Jetty Lynn Carmichael (me) is definitely interesting.

November 6

Mrs. Taylor told me it was time to meet with Mrs. B again.

Mrs. B gave me a special pass to use when I need to.

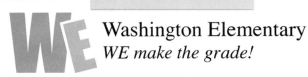

Washington Elementary
WE make the grade!

STUDENT HALL PASS

Name: Jetty Lynn Carmichael
Grade: 4
Teacher: Mrs. Taylor

Hall Pass must be carried at all times.

So now we are making a plan to help me out.

Here is what we have to do. First, to help me get my homework done.

From the desk of *Mrs. B.*

Supplies for Study Area

- Sharpened Pencils
- Erasers
- Markers
- Ruler
- Paper
- Dictionary
- Timer

1. My own study area with all my supplies ready to go.

No searching during study time!

I can't wait to make my study place.

 Mrs. B says no more working on the floor by the TV.

 Homework is my job.

 No TV or phone calls.

 Quiet music is okay.

No words in the song.
It makes me sing.

Singing + Math Problems = Wacky Answers!

Student at Work!

Do NOT Disturb!

2. A study schedule for each day
   with a break for me.

Study Schedule

3:30 - 4:00 PM: Snack/Get out homework

4:00 - 4:20 PM: Reading

4:20 - 4:25 PM: Break!

4:30 - 4:45 PM: Science questions

4:45 - 4:50 PM: Break!

4:50 - 5:10 PM: Write spelling words 2x each

5:15 PM: Clean up and put homework away

6:00 PM: Dinner!

3. Use my planner every day. Get it signed.

4. Get help from my homework buddy.

5. Use my school bin by the front door for all
   my stuff going back to school the next day.

   No more family scavenger hunts.
       (And no more Katie Kazoo disasters.)

NOVEMBER

12 Monday

Write spelling words 2x
Practice 5 times tables

13 Tuesday

Read 20 minutes
Science questions

14 Wednesday

Write vocab sentences
Read 20 minutes

15 Thursday

Study for spelling test
Math flash cards
Read 20 minutes

16 Friday

Write summary about
main idea of book

x _CarrieAnn Carmichael_

November 7

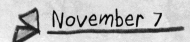 **ALL ABOUT** 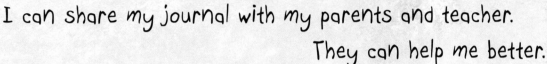 *Jetty*

Dr. petrie likes it that I have a journal.

 Writing about my feelings helps.

I can share my journal with my parents and teacher.

They can help me better.

Today will be a good day.

MEET the

NEW

improved

JETTY.

Jetty's Journal

Eeeek!

Stuff I DON'T Like

- Girlie-girls, movie-star girls.
  They are so not fun.
  They stay clean all the time.
  They squeal in the rain.
  They don't jump in puddles.
  And they like to shop. Blecch!
  They do boring things for fun.

- Dolls are for girlie-girls.

- And pink things stink.

Shop!

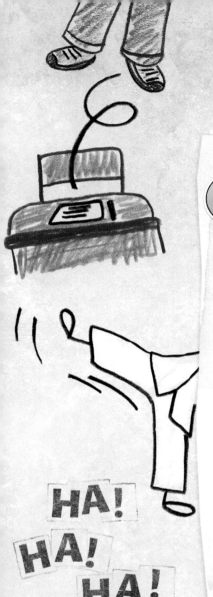

 I'd rather hang out with Jordan.
Jordan and Jetty. We could be twins.
Except we don't look alike.

He never pays attention.
And he has his own work mountain.

He really does spring out of his seat.
He falls on the floor!

 He is hilarious!

He karate kicks all the time.
(when the teacher is not looking)

 We ride bikes after school.

HA!
HA!
HA!

Oops! I forgot to write about what I DON'T like.

• Cursive writing (but guess what? My teacher
is letting me do some of my work on
the computer! Woo Hoo!)

Mrs. Taylor wants us to tell more about ourselves.
Here goes! I forgot...

I do NOT like

> Super annoying...giggly whispering girls.
> They're always making fun of me.
> And they're not nice.

Important things to know about me...

- I can't sit still. There's a flip flopping inside of me. And I need to move.
- Everyone says I fidget. (funny word) It means I make a lot of little movements. Dad calls me his Fidget Widget.
- I'm a nail picker.
- And a knuckle cracker. (Mom hates that.)
- Even my pencils are tap dancers. (I miss my sparkly one.)
- I love to do cartwheels. *
- I even talk in non-stop action. Mom says I'm a chatterbox.

*Note to Self: Show Dr. Petrie my new deluxe cartwheel.

Today I am supposed to tell you how I feel inside at school.

My outside self is WAY different from my inside self.

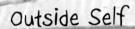

Outside Self	Inside self
Smiles and laughs	Worries no one likes me
Friendly	Thinks no one will be my friend
Chatty	Thinks no one listens to me
Confident	Feels like the other kids are smarter than me

November 9

I have Major Meltdowns!
And that reminds me... We studied volcanoes.

I am Jetty,
the Human Volcano.

Angry feelings = molten lava
Hot and burning.

Once the feelings start to move up
there's no stopping them.
My anger gushes out like a volcano erupting.
I yell, I cry, I lose control.
It takes me a long time to feel better.

But volcanoes don't feel ashamed
afterwards. Jetty, the Human Volcano,
gets embarrassed.

Mrs. B said molten lava feelings creep up on you.
And erupt before you know it.

If I had a giant fan,

I could cool down the feelings

before they erupt.

That is what Time Out is for.
And counting to 10.

 Mrs. B likes my inside/outside chart.
She wants me to write about things I like.

 I want her to write about
things she likes.

Then we compare!

November 12

Today I write about things I like.
I don't like too much stuff.

THINGS I LIKE

- Animals
- Hula hoops
- Beef jerky
- Playing tag with Jordan
- Cookies
- Pizza
- Fake tattoos
- Karate
- Helping the teacher

YOU'RE IT!

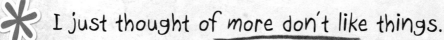 I just thought of <u>more</u> don't like things.

- Dresses
- purses
- Headbands and scrunchies
- When people tell me to turn
  my volume down like I'm a TV
  or something. It's embarrassing.

Mrs. B didn't have the same things on her chart that I did. Not even beef jerky.

She had books and flowers and singing and other stuff.

But I like her anyway.

You don't have to like the same things.

That's what Mrs. B said.

We can share our "likes" with each other. But we don't have to be exactly the same.

Today we had to write about our favorite day.

I don't have a favorite day, but. . .if I did,
my favorite day would be if

- I don't have to walk in a straight line.
- I have NO homework.
- I have a best friend.
- I don't lose anything.
- No one yells at me.
- Nobody bothers me.

 My Unfavorite days...
When the teasers make fun
of me for no reason.

I want to talk about...

TEASERS

Teasers are kind of mean.

- They make fun of me when I get in trouble.
- Or they smile a mean smile.
- They don't let me play sometimes.

*  They know how to make me mad and lose control.

 Even though I never do anything bad to them.

November 15

OK. I admit it. Sometimes I hurt people's feelings.
But they start it first.

Like today, Brent sharpens his pencils during
Reading AGAIN!

Am I the only kid who knows the rules?

I yell at him.
Guess who gets in trouble? Hint: It's not Brent.
It isn't fair. I get real mad at Mrs. Taylor.

WE Washington Elementary
WE make the grade!

DISCIPLINARY REFERRAL

Student Name: Jetty Lynn Carmichael
Grade: 4
Date: November 15

Reason(s) for Referral:
- ☐ Disruptive behavior
- ☐ Inappropriate language
- ☐ Inappropriate dress
- ☑ Rude/discourteous behavior
- ☐ Fighting
- ☐ Tardiness
- ☐ Other _____

Teacher's signature: Mrs. Taylor
Principal's signature: Mr. Schroeder

She wants me to
go to Time Out
to cool down.

I won't go. Kids
are looking at me.

I have to go talk
to Mr. Schroeder.
I never had to
go to the
principal before.

Mr. Schroeder has to call my mother.
I was rude to my teacher.
I didn't mean to be.

I got nervous.
Everyone was staring at me.
I said "No" before my brain
 thought about it.

Now I'm in trouble at home and in school.

I have to write an "I'm sorry" note to Mrs. Taylor.

Mrs. Taylor,

I'm sorry for not going to Time Out.
I will try to control myself better in
class and be more respectful.

I hope you will accept my apology.

Sincerely,
Jetty Lynn Carmichael

Jetty's ~~First~~ Last Very Sad Trip to the Principal

Sitting in a big chair
all by myself.
A little tear starts but I sniff it back.

Mr. Schroeder talks to me.
He sits at a big desk.

My voice sounds tiny.
I'm feeling very sorry about being
rude to Mrs. Taylor.

I didn't mean it.

I wish I could think before I speak.

Then I wouldn't be here.
 I'd be at recess with my class.

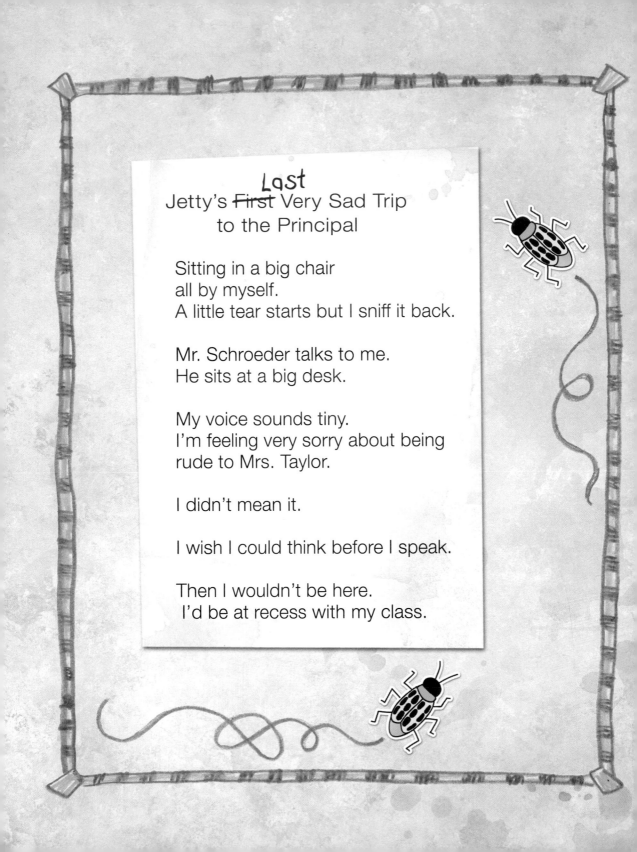

November 16

I want to be a regular kid.

Mrs. B says it will help if I make some goals.

Not football goals!
Goals that will help me be happier.

JETTY'S HAPPINESS GOALS

1. Get a best friend.
   (Not a girlie-girl.)
2. Stay out of trouble.
3. Get better grades.

November 19

Mrs. B helped me think of some ideas to help me with my goals. We typed them up.

1. **Get a best friend:**

    - Look for friends that like the same stuff I do, like karate, animals, bikes.

    - Be friendly. Listen. Don't try to do all the talking.

    - Give compliments. Be myself.

    - Enjoy differences between us.

2. **Stay out of trouble:**

    Try to relieve stress in class by:

    - Deep breathing (that means taking in a big breath, holding it, and breathing out slowly)

    - Counting to 10

    - Talking to someone (parents, teacher, counselor)

    - Finding a place at school where I can go to calm down

Places I can go:

- Mrs. B's office.

- The Quiet Zone in our class.

- My teacher from third grade said I could work at a desk in her class.

- The teacher next door.

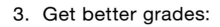

3. Get better grades:

- Get to school on time

- Write assignments in planner

- Get parents and teacher to sign

- Stick to my homework schedule

- Talk to my homework buddy

- Organize study area

- Clean out desk and backpack

- Take home everything that does not belong at school

November 20

Mrs. B made me a chart to keep track of my organization goal.

I go see Mrs. B each afternoon.

Start off each day with a Bang!!

1. Be at school on time.
2. Empty backpack.
3. Put away backpack and lunch.
4. Turn in homework to tray.
5. Complete Morning "Do Now."
6. Get ready for Reading.
7. Be on the right page during lessons.
8. Follow directions.
9. TCOJ ("Take Care of Jetty!")
10. Use planner to write homework and reminders.

I want to earn 10 points every day.

Mrs. B says if I start off my day organized it will help me the rest of the day.

Start off each day with a Bang!!

- [ ] 1. Be at school on time. *Keep trying!*
- [x] 2. Empty backpack.
- [ ] 3. Put away backpack and lunch. *Be sure to put backpack away.*
- [x] 4. Turn in homework to tray.
- [x] 5. Complete Morning "Do Now." ☺
- [ ] 6. Get ready for Reading. *Don't forget your workbook.*
- [ ] 7. Be on the right page during lessons.
- [ ] 8. Follow directions. *Listen carefully!* *Almost there.*
- [x] 9. TCOJ ("Take Care of Jetty!") ☺
- [x] 10. Use planner to write homework and reminders. *Super!*

⟹ Just **5** points today.

Mrs. B said that was a good try.
We are going to work on the other 5.

<u>December 3</u>

Medicine Madness

Today is my first Medicine Day. Dr. Petrie said the medicine would help me focus. Swallowing pills makes me throw up.
Does she know that?

First we tried a pill + water.

Gag!

Mom wraps a pill in cheese. (It works for my dog!)
My tongue finds it.

Pill + applesauce.
"CRUNCH!" I bite on it. "BLECCH!"
Bitter, bitter, bitter!

Mom gets a new pill and mixes it with cookie dough ice cream. Mmmm! Sweet success!

I'm the only kid I know that has ice cream right after breakfast.

I don't know why Mom is so tired.
I'm the one who's doing all the swallowing.

December 5

It's kind of strange. Today is Pizza Day in the cafeteria.

 I always buy pizza. Pizza is my LIFE.

Cheese pizza, I mean.

Washington Elementary
WE make the grade!

December
Lunch Menu

MONDAY	TUESDAY	WEDNESDAY	THURSDAY	FRIDAY
3 Dog Nuggets Roll Pear Slices Milk Selection	**4** Chili with Beef Roll Fruit Cup Milk Selection	**5** Pizza Salad Applesauce Milk Selection	**6** Oriental Chicken Rice Steamed Broccoli Milk Selection	**7** Macaroni & Cheese Mixed Vegetable Banana Milk Selection
10 Cheeseburger on a Bun Steamed Vegetables Apple Milk Selection	**11** Grilled Cheese Sandwich Vegetable Soup Apple Milk Selection	**12** Popcorn Chicken Roll Corn Milk Selection	**13** Cheese Ravioli Roll Grapes Milk Selection	**14** Beef Burrito Steamed Rice Fruit Cup Milk Selection
18			20	21

But today I'm not hungry.
My tummy hurts.

After school I'm starving.
I want to eat everything in the whole fridge.

December 6

I'm not hungry again at lunch.
I eat my apple and just one cookie.

Guess What? When I get home, I'm so hungry
I eat 2 PB and J sandwiches.

I even eat dinner after that. But then I can't fall asleep.

Tick
Tock
Tick
Tock

Nights are very long
when you're awake.
And very short when
you're asleep.

What's going on?
Is it my new medicine?

Some nights I could eat 5 pizzas by myself. Really!

Jetty Carmichael:
World Famous Pizza
Eating Machine!

x5

December 10

Interim Report Time is here.

I'm trying hard.
But no Honor Roll.

And it says
Needs Improvement.

I thought my
medicine would
help me get
better grades.

What's up
with that?

WE — Washington Elementary
WE make the grade!

Student Name: Jetty Lynn Carmichael
Teacher: Taylor
Grade: 4

QUARTER:	__ 1st	X 2nd	__ 3rd	__4th

SOCIAL GROWTH

Shows self-control	MS
Works cooperatively	MS
Respects authority	NI
Respects rights and property of others	MS

STUDY SKILLS

Stays on task	NI
Follows directions	MS
Completes assignments on time	MS
Brings necessary materials to class	NI

ATTENDANCE

Attends school regularly	ES
Attends school on time	NI

Key: ES = Exceeds Standards
MS = Meets Standards
NI = Needs Improvement

Mrs. B says it takes time. We just have to keep trying.

Waiting is hard. I want it to work yesterday!

December 14

Guess What?

Christmas is coming.
I am working on my list.
More waiting.

Jetty's Christmas List

- A best friend
- New bike
- Sparkly pencil
- Animal books
- An ant farm
- A puppy
- A horse
- New sneakers

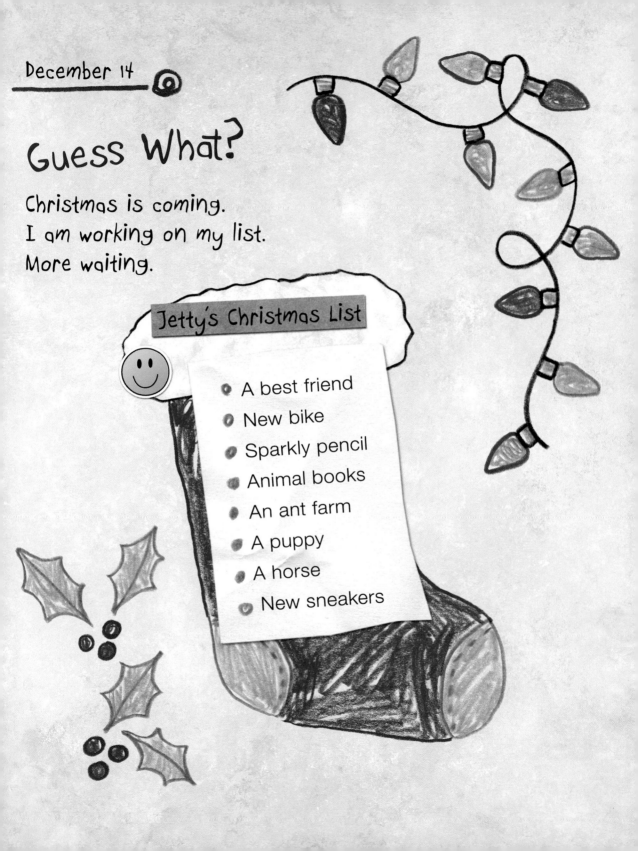

December 17

Today, my teacher said to write the things
I'm good at. I can't remember any.
 Mrs. Taylor helped me.

I'm a super athlete.
I help other kids at reading.
 I read with expression.
I zip through my twelve times tables.

Name _Jetty Lynn Carmichael_

MATH

12 TIMES TABLE

12 x 1   = 12
12 x 2   = 24
12 x 3   = 36
12 x 4   = 48
12 x 5   = 60
12 x 6   = 72
12 x 7   = 84
12 x 8   = 96
12 x 9   = 108
12 x 10 = 120

I dance like
nobody's business.
I got the moves.

I know lots
of facts
about
animals.

Wow. I **AM** good at stuff. **LOTSA** stuff.

That's a surprise!

So if there are lots of things I'm good at, how come all I can think about are the things I stink at?

Things like:

- Listening.
- Following directions.
- Keeping my hands to myself.
- Finishing work.
- Doing chores.

Who has time to think about the good things?

 Merry Christmas!   No problem getting up
early on Christmas!

No puppy or horse but I did get some cool animal books.

And the new bike I wanted!!   **Woo Hoo!**

PS. I didn't really think I would get
an ant farm. Even though I ask for
one every year.

I still need to find a best friend, though.

January 7

Back to school. Great.

My Winter Break

Here's what I did:
- practiced karate
- decorated cookies with Dad
- visited Grandma
- rode bikes with Jordan
  (and tried my new bike!)
- went to the movies with Mom

January 8

We have to write some New Year's Resolutions.
They are like my goals.

Jetty's New Year's Resolutions

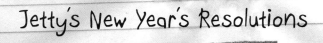 1. Pay attention.

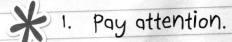 2. Make Mom and Dad proud.

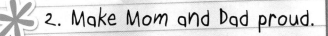 3. Don't forget stuff.

January 14

Mrs. Taylor showed me my goals sheet again.

→ I am going to work on my TCOJ goal tomorrow.
→ And following directions.
→

Start off each day with a **Bang!!**

- ☑ 1. Be at school on time.
- ☑ 2. Empty backpack.
- ☑ 3. Put away backpack and lunch.
- ☑ 4. Turn in homework to tray.   *Wow!*
- ☑ 5. Complete Morning "Do Now." ☺
- ☐ 6. Get ready for Reading. *Don't forget your workbook.*
- ☑ 7. Be on the right page during lessons.
- ☐ 8. Follow directions. *Pay attention during reading.*
- ☐ 9. TCOJ ("Take Care of Jetty!") *Keep Trying!*
- ☑ 10. Use planner to write homework ☺ and reminders.

January 17

Big News!

We are going on a field trip to the zoo.
I can't wait to see the big cats.

 WOW!

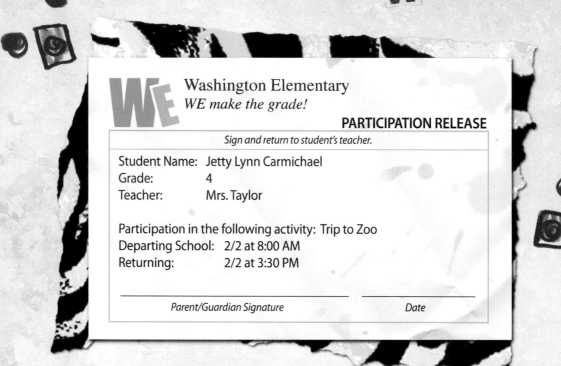

Washington Elementary
WE make the grade!

PARTICIPATION RELEASE

Sign and return to student's teacher.

Student Name: Jetty Lynn Carmichael
Grade: 4
Teacher: Mrs. Taylor

Participation in the following activity: Trip to Zoo
Departing School: 2/2 at 8:00 AM
Returning: 2/2 at 3:30 PM

_____   _____
Parent/Guardian Signature   Date

I am always waiting! I wish the trip was tomorrow.

I know a lot about animals.
Cheetahs can run 45 miles per hour.

Field trips are awesome. No work for us that day!

@ January 21

Another barfy breakfast. Eggs!
  I still don't feel like eating lunch.

Yuck!

Mom says I have to go back to Dr. Petrie to see
if my medicine is why I don't feel like eating
breakfast or lunch.

And maybe it keeps me awake.

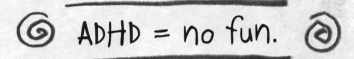
@ ADHD = no fun. @

I'm tired of going to the doctor. It's boring.
And I don't know why I take this medicine.
 It doesn't work. It makes me hungry, keeps me awake,
and my grades NEED IMPROVEMENT.

Does that
sound like
it's working?

FAMILY MEDICAL CLINIC
Isabel Petrie, MD

Jetty Lynn
has an appointment
MON (TUES) WED THUR FRI SAT
January 29   at *4:30 pm*
40 Washington Square WILDWOOD 555-0189

I don't think so!
I'm waiting to tell the
doctor it's not working.

 Waiting all the time is unfair and cruel to kids.

Report Card again. Mine still says Needs Improvement.

And it even says I might have to go to summer school.

Summer school = Bummer school

Washington Elementary
WE make the grade!

Student Name: Jetty Lynn Carmichael
Teacher: Taylor
Grade: 4

	1st	2nd	3rd	4th
SOCIAL GROWTH				
Shows self-control	MS	MS		
Works cooperatively	MS	MS		
Respects authority	NI	NI		
Respects rights and property of others	MS	MS		
STUDY SKILLS				
Stays on task	NI	MS		
Follows directions	MS	NI		
Completes assignments on time	MS	MS		
Brings necessary materials to class	NI	NI		
ATTENDANCE				
Attends school regularly	ES	ES		
Attends school on time	NI	NI		

Comments:
Student may be required to attend Summer School

Key: ES = Exceeds Standards
MS = Meets Standards
NI = Needs Improvement

Summer is vacation time.

ADHD means no vacation for Jetty.

I think I'm over this ADHD stuff.

February 2

The zoo field trip was fun! The bus ride was sooo long. The bus driver kept telling me to sit down. I was excited.

There were a gazillion animals.

My favorite = monkeys.

Crazy wild acrobats. I'm pretty sure monkeys have ADHD.

My next favorite part was the aviary, where the birds are.

I'm positive birds are ADHD.

Hummingbirds for sure.

MAYES ZOO
AND AQUARIUM COMPLEX

STUDENT TICKET

Become a Mayes Zoo Friend and receive membership discounts!

ZOO HOURS
9:00 a.m. to 5:00 p.m.
DAILY

Ticket valid day of admission only.

My best field trip ever.

It was zoo-riffic!

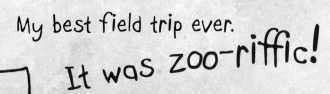

February 4

Guess what? Breakfast is looking better.

No more eggs and hot cereal
and yucchy breakfast stuff.

 B is for
Better Breakfasts

 Mom Is
AMAZING!

Mom's New and Improved Breakfast Menu

 New Breakfast Choices!

NOW SERVING:
- Hamburger or cheeseburger
- Chicken sandwich
- PB and J
- Yogurt and fruit and granola

 MOM makes
breakfast
better!

My stomach likes this menu. And it's still good for me.

February 6

Dr. Petrie adjusted my medicine.
   It worked!
What a difference!

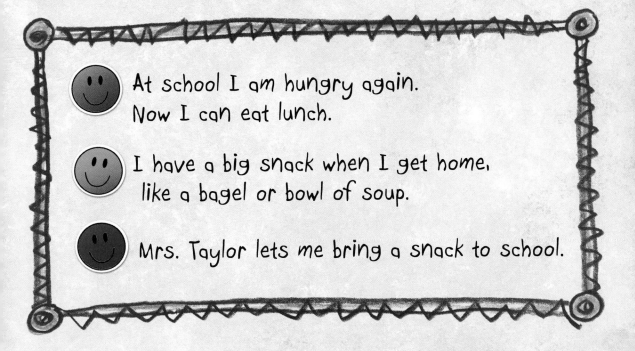

At school I am hungry again.
Now I can eat lunch.

I have a big snack when I get home,
   like a bagel or bowl of soup.

Mrs. Taylor lets me bring a snack to school.

And I can fall asleep better. Mom and Dad like that a lot.

A whole lot!

February 14

HAPPY VALENTINE'S DAY!

Party!
Valentines!
Snacks!
Games!

WILD ABOUT YOU!

Happy Valentine's Day!
Love ya,
Mom & Dad

I love Valentine's Day.

 But even better, tonight is karate!
We are going to learn roundhouse kicks.

Valentines + Karate = Super Fun!

February 15

Today is a 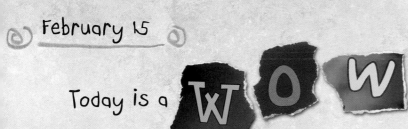 day.

I keep getting checkmarks on my chart.

I'm feeling FOCUSED! I think, maybe, I will get 10 points.

→
→
→
But 9 points for me. Jayden was sharpening during Math. I told on him. Mrs. Taylor reminded me about TCOJ. (And it means Take Care of Jetty, not Jayden!)

Mrs. B said I did very well anyway. She gave me an award. **Yay!**

WOW!

Good Behavior Award

Awarded to

Jetty Lynn Carmichael

February 15
Date

Mrs. B
Signature

I have some good news!

I have a friend! A karate friend.

Mandy is coming over to my house over spring break.
We are going to practice roundhouse kicks.

Karate + roundhouse kicks = friendship

 Mrs. B said that it is good to have friends that share interests with you.

We both really want to test for our YELLOW belts!  That's for sure.

March 20

Yesterday I got all  points on my chart.

Mrs. Taylor was proud.

Mrs. B was proud.

Mom and Dad were proud.

I was proud.

 WAY TO GO!

I think the whole world was proud.

Our family celebrated.

 HURRAY!

April 1

I am really getting the hang of fourth grade.

Homework isn't as bad now that I
have a plan. Sometimes Mandy and
I do homework together.

Plus there is a new girl in my class. Rachael.
Mrs. Taylor picked me to be her buddy.

Now, Rachael is in my karate class too.
I have best friends
coming out of my ears. Jordan and

Rachael and

Mandy.

First I have NO friends.

Now Jetty + 3 = 4 BFF.

P.S. None of this is
an April Fool's joke.

April 4

We are getting ready for our state tests.
I am kind of scared.

 You have to pass them to go to fifth grade.

 What if I don't pass?
What if I never pass?

Then I will be in fourth grade the rest of my life.
Even when I'm really old. Like 30.

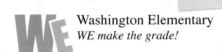

WE Washington Elementary
WE make the grade!

Dear Parents,
Fourth graders will be given state assessments in language arts on
April 15-16 and mathematics on April 22-23.

Make-up tests will be held the week of April 29.

Results will be available in May.

Sincerely,
Mr. Schroeder
Mr. Schroeder
Principal

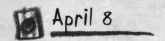 <u>April 8</u>

Testing time!

We practice and practice.

Tests make you really tired. One day I almost fell asleep on my desk.

 ZᶻZᶻz

In tests you have to stay focused.

And use all your strategies.

And check your work.

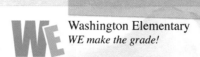

WE Washington Elementary
WE make the grade!

Fourth Grade State Assessments
SCHEDULE

MONDAY APRIL 15
  10:00-10:45 AM   Reading
  Extra long recess

TUESDAY APRIL 16
  10:00-10:45 AM   Grammar and punctuation
  Extra long recess

MONDAY APRIL 22
  10:00-10:45 AM   Math
  Extra long recess

TUESDAY APRIL 23
  10:00-10:45 AM   Math
  Extra long recess

Parents—Please see that your child is well rested before tests.

Whew! That's a lot for a kid in fourth grade.

April 10

I think I am doing better.

It's a secret. I didn't tell anyone.
If they know, it might not be true.

SHHHH!

 But I think I am paying
attention better.

 And listening better.

 GOOD JOB! WOW!

And following the rules
better. Sometimes!

I don't know if it is the medicine,
or if it is me trying harder.

 It's probably me. I am trying hard!!!

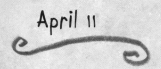

April 11

Is it just me? Or do I feel more calm?
Things don't make me so mad.
And I feel happier at school.

Mrs. Taylor gives me compliments.

Good work on your test, Jetty.

I like the way you paid attention.

Thank you for helping me clean up.

Sometimes compliments are embarrassing. I have to get used to them.

April 25

I haven't had Journal Time for a while
  because of testing. But here I am again.
  I have great news.
        I mean REALLY TERRIFIC!

So good I am using some of my special Jetty Confetti!

Yesterday was Conference Day!
All you need to know is one word. Just one!

We have been working on 3 things.
1. Completing work
2. Talking to someone when I have a problem.
3. Following directions.

 Now that I'm doing better,
        I even noticed that school
        is more fun.

Home is more fun too.
My chore chart means I don't forget to do my chores.

Jetty's Chores

WEEK OF APRIL 23

	MON	TUE	WED	THUR	FRI	SAT	SUN
put away clothes	😊	😊	⭐				
make bed	😊	😊					
feed cat		😊	⭐				
take medicine	😊	😊	⭐				

I am pretty good at doing my homework.
   Sometimes Mom has to help me but I am in charge.

I stay on task. Yay. That's the hardest part.

April 29

You're not going to believe this.

Mrs. Taylor made ME the Teacher Helper for this week.

She said that now that I am taking charge of more of my learning, I can help other kids with their reading.

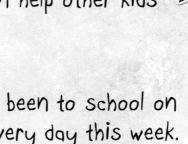

I have been to school on time every day this week.
It's because I get all organized the night before.

Jetty's
School Stuff

Then I don't have to catch up on my Do-Now work when I get to school.

Work Mountain has disappeared!

Mrs. Taylor gave me a reward from her Teacher Box.

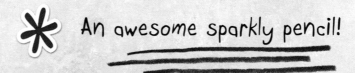

* An awesome sparkly pencil!

And I'm getting better grades.
Even my handwriting seems better.
Mrs. Taylor can read it.

Jetty Lynn Carmichael
Grade 4
Mrs. Taylor
April 24

Spring is awesome
Spring is cool.
Outside flowers are blooming.
And I am stuck in school!

Nice Work!

 No more Jetty Volcano.

My good feelings are stronger now.

 Even the Teasers are on vacation.

✳ I still get mad. But I know what I can do about it.

I like being in control of myself.

May 3

News of the day!

I am invited to Rachael's birthday party.

I can't wait. More waiting!

Jordan and Mandy are going too.

It's a **Birthday Party!**

Mandy and I are promoted
in karate and we earn our YELLOW belts.

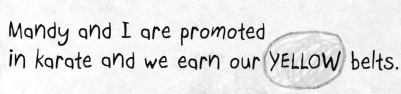

High five to us! We rock!

Mrs. Taylor writes a good note
to Mom and Dad.
I am so excited.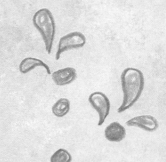

But then it gets lost.

I start to get a tear in my eye but Mrs. Taylor
makes me a new one. (Wonderful teacher.)

Star
Student!
Awarded to:

Jetty Lynn Carmichael

Jetty has shown great
improvement in school. It is
a pleasure having her in class!

Mrs. Taylor

I still need
a little help.
But that's OK!

June 3

I am going over to Mandy's house this weekend for my first sleepover.

It's a Sleepover!

Mom and I are practicing how to behave.

Say please and thank you

Cooperate and share

Talk in a soft voice

Use good manners at dinner

Flush the toilet (sometimes I forget)

June 5

I have my last report card. I hold my breath and look.

I am promoted to Fifth Grade.

No Summer School.

I dance a little Jetty Jig. Mrs. Taylor laughs.

I'm going to miss her next year.
But at least I know how to help myself now.

I think the rest of my goals
 are going to be easy-peasey.

But I'll tell you one thing.
No kid should ever have to write in complete sentences.

Note to Readers

As you read through *Get Ready for Jetty,* did Jetty's life sound familiar? Part of being a writer is doing research to make sure that my character becomes real to my readers. My research was tons of fun. I interviewed different girls in elementary school who had AD/HD. Their comments helped me to create Jetty's great personality. I discovered some strengths and weaknesses my main character might have in school and at home. And I realized something important. Each girl is an individual. AD/HD can look quite different from person to person.

So what if you find out you have AD/HD? Or what if you know someone else who does? There are lots of successful strategies that can help kids deal with the challenges of AD/HD. It all begins with teamwork.

Building a Support Team

It is important to have a great support team for assistance in making progress toward your goals. You and your parents will need to understand about AD/HD. You will read about it, hear about it, and talk to other people about it.

Once you understand what this whole AD/HD thing is all about, you'll work with your support team. The good part is that you don't have to do it alone. You might require a little extra help from each member of your team for a while, but you will figure it out for yourself as time goes by. Here are some of the people you might have on your support team:

Your parents. Your parents are the first team members. Parents need to communicate regularly with your teacher(s) to keep things running smoothly at school. They can check your work at night and make sure you're on track. They help monitor your medicine, if that is part of your treatment plan. They also take you to the doctor regularly to make sure you are in good health.

Your teacher. Most teachers use daily planners or e-mail to communicate with parents. Your teacher may want to have private talks with you to help you. She can guide you in setting goals and helping you chart your progress. Talk to your teacher about the rules and routines in the classroom. Your teacher can give you a little secret signal, like a thumbs up, when you remember to follow the rules. She may keep a checklist for you on how you are doing at staying focused, or on task. This helps you know how you are doing each day.

Your homework buddy. A homework buddy is a classmate who helps you out in school. You and your homework buddy can make sure that you both have what you need to do your homework each night. You can also exchange phone numbers and call each other if you have questions about the homework or to ask what you need to bring to school the next day.

Your doctor. Your pediatrician is a member of your support team, too.

Regular visits to the doctor will be an important part of your treatment. Your doctor can give you information about AD/HD that will help you to understand what to expect. Your family and your doctor may feel you need some medicine to help you focus. The doctor makes sure that you take the proper medicine in the right amount for your age and size.

Your school counselor. Another member of your support team works at your school. It might be helpful to talk to another adult besides your teacher, so talk to your school counselor about problems or concerns you may be having. School counselors understand you may be feeling anxious or upset. They know all about stress and how to relieve it. And they are great at celebrating successes with you. Sometimes they will suggest that you meet with other kids to talk together. Group support can be really helpful.

Your therapist. Sometimes, kids with AD/HD might need some extra help from a therapist. A therapist is someone whose job is to talk to you about your thoughts and feelings, and work with you to figure out a plan to help things get better in your life. A therapist can be a social worker, psychologist, or psychiatrist. They work with many other kids with AD/HD just like you. You can be honest with your therapist about your feelings, and he or she will not tell anyone else—not even your parents. Their job is to listen to you and help you figure out what to do about the things that are bothering you. Sometimes your therapist might meet with your parents to give them some helpful advice, too.

You! The most important member of the support team is…*Guess who?* Of course, it is *you.* Without your cooperation and positive attitude, it will be hard to achieve your goals. You are the captain of your team!

Now, I'd like to give you some tips on getting organized, dealing with your feelings, making friends, thinking positively, and focusing on your strengths—stuff that is important and can really help you.

Getting Organized

Not being organized can be very frustrating. If you can't find your school supplies, then you have to borrow them from other kids or do without. Important notices can get lost—like those permission slips for awesome field trips. It is very annoying when you work hard to complete your homework and find out the next day that it must have escaped from your backpack somehow. Not to mention that parents get quite a bit upset when you can't find what you need for the day!

So an organization plan is really important. It helps to oversee all the other snags that can come with AD/HD (like learning to manage time, pay attention, get help that you need). What would this plan look like?

At School
- Leave things at home that do not belong at school.
- Follow all parts of the morning procedure. Check them off.
- Use a daily planner to record assignments.

- Get assistance from a homework buddy.
- Clean out your desk weekly. Keep papers in folders.
- Check your backpack to see if you have all your homework.

At Home: Chores
- Use a chore chart to mark off what you need to do at home.
- Write notes for a "To Do" list and check off completed items.

At Home: Homework
- Create an organized and complete study area.
- Make sure your homework area is free from interruptions.
- Set up a homework schedule for each day.
- Make sure you have everything you need before you start.
- Prioritize your assignments.
- Use a timer.
- Add a short break between subjects to stretch.
- Check off each assignment as you complete it.
- Have your parents check your homework and sign your planner.
- Clean up your study area for the next day.
- Pack up your backpack and put school items in a bin by the door.
- Celebrate a job well done!

Dealing With Feelings

Feelings can really get in the way of learning and making friends. Life can feel like a rocky roller coaster ride. Some students come to school upset and they are out of sorts all day. Some kids are calm and happy until something makes them angry. They may erupt like a volcano, and it may ruin the rest of their day. One thing is for sure. You cannot concentrate on school when you are not feeling good about your day.

It is always helpful to talk about your feelings with someone—whether that is your parents, grandparents, a favorite aunt or uncle, your teacher, or school counselor. You can also talk to a therapist, whose job is to listen and help you figure out a plan to deal with things that are bothering you. Talking with someone will help you feel better and understand why you feel the way you do. If you have a hard time talking about your feelings, remember that it gets easier with practice. You may try keeping a journal, like Jetty does. It's kind of like talking to yourself, but writing in a journal can help you sort through your thoughts and feelings.

Making Friends

Friends are an important part of school (and life!). Friendship comes easily to some, but not to others. Many girls with AD/HD have lots of friends—they have a good sense of humor and are fun to be around. Sometimes girls with AD/HD may prefer to play with boys rather than girls, and that's okay. However, some girls with AD/HD find it more difficult to make or keep friends. They may feel different from other kids in their class or worry that others don't like them. Remember that you have lots of positive qualities and that finding a good friend can take time.

Friends can be found in other areas besides school. If you are involved in scouting, or karate, or other group activities, you may find some girls, or even boys, who share similar interests with you. Remember, to make friends you must be a good friend, too. That means you need to listen, be supportive, be friendly, and give compliments. Like everything else, being a good friend can take practice!

Thinking Positively

Attitude is everything! Use your best "calming down" tricks to slow down and think before you act or speak. Counting to 10 works great for some kids. Others go to a quiet place to refocus. Some kids even write down what they are upset about. Sometimes just writing it down releases the angry feelings! Do whatever it takes. Get control of your behavior! Don't let it control you!

Practice thinking in positive ways. Turn your negative thoughts around into positive ones. Instead of thinking:
I hate getting up so early to go to school.
Try:
Morning is not my best time but the good thing is that I get out earlier!

Instead of:
I stink at Math and Science.
Try:
I'm doing really good in Reading and Spelling. Maybe Mom and Dad can help me in Math and Science.

Instead of:
Nobody likes me.
Try:
What could I do to be a good friend?

Focusing on Your Strengths

Kids with AD/HD are just as smart and talented as other kids. In addition, there are lots of wonderful things that may come with having AD/HD. You may have a great sense of humor, or be very enthusiastic or creative. Perhaps you are good at drama, music, or sports. You may have lots of energy and curiosity, and make life more interesting for others around you. Because you know that sometimes it's hard to be a little different, you may be sensitive and helpful to others who need a friend.

It might be useful to make a list of all your strengths and weaknesses. Everybody has strengths as well as weaknesses! Once you have listed your strengths, think about some areas you would like to improve. You may find that you will be able to use your strengths to help balance out other areas.

The most important thing to remember is that AD/HD is not who you are, it is just a small part of you. Focus on what you can do, not what you can't do. The rest will come.